Bug Patrol

LOOKING FOR BUTTERFLIES

Written by

EMILIE DUFRESNE

KidHaven
PUBLISHING

Published in 2023 by KidHaven Publishing,
an Imprint of Greenhaven Publishing, LLC
29 East 21st Street
New York, NY 10010

Edited by:
Madeline Tyler

Designed by:
Brandon Mattless

Cataloging-in-Publication Data

Names: Dufresne, Emilie.
Title: Looking for butterflies / Emilie Dufresne.
Description: New York : KidHaven Publishing, 2023. | Series: Bug patrol | Includes glossary and index.
Identifiers: ISBN 9781534541214 (pbk.) | ISBN 9781534541238 (library bound) | ISBN 9781534541221 (6 pack) | ISBN 9781534541245 (ebook)
Subjects: LCSH: Butterflies--Juvenile literature.
Classification: LCC QL544.2 D84 2023 | DDC 595.78'9--dc23

Manufactured in the United States of America

CPSIA compliance information: Batch #CSKH23: For further information contact Greenhaven Publishing LLC, New York, New York at 1-844-317-7404.

Please visit our website, www.greenhavenpublishing.com.
For a free color catalog of all our high-quality books,
call toll free 1-844-317-7404 or fax 1-844-317-7405.

Photo Credits

All images are courtesy of Shutterstock.com, unless otherwise specified. With thanks to Getty Images, Thinkstock Photo and iStockphoto.
Front Cover – Chinnapong, Le Do, pranee_stocker, Production Perig, musicman. Recurring Images – Andrey Pavlov, rangizzz, Valentyn Volkov, musicman, artproem, Filip Dokladal, Paladin12. 4–5 – all_about_people, Butterfly Hunter, Jacob Lund. 6–7 – Africa Studio, Sarycheva Olesia, sutham, TheFarAwayKingdom. 8–9 – anek.soowannaphoom, DutchScenery, stockyimages. 10–11 – Amrit Raj, ArtYouAre, fotosutra, Marco Uliana. 12–13 – Don Williamson, Epiglottis, Gallinago_media, photomaster. 14–15 – David Benton, Keith Hider, Stephan Morris. 16–17 – aaltair, Alistair Hobbs, Paul Stringer. 18–19 – Cristina Romero Palma, MRS. NUCH SRIBUANOY, Pieter Bruin. 20–21 – ips, Mateusz Sciborski, Mirko Graul.

CONTENTS

Words that look like **this** can be found in the glossary on page 24.

GO OUTSIDE!

The world is full of amazing creatures! What creatures can you find?

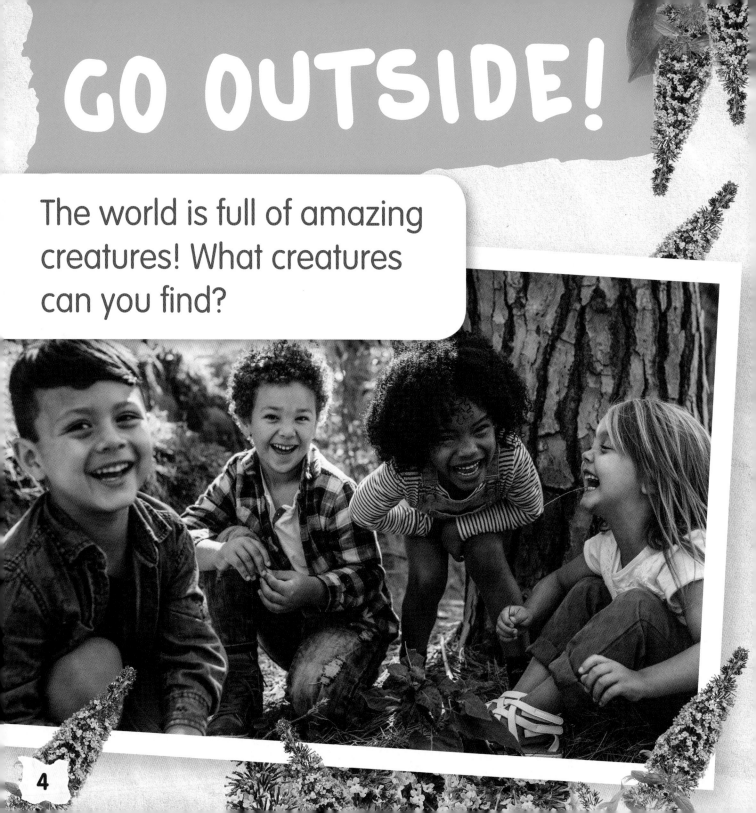

Go outside and see what butterflies you can find!

BE READY!

Make sure you are ready to explore.

You will need:

Magnifying glass

A snack

Waterproof boots

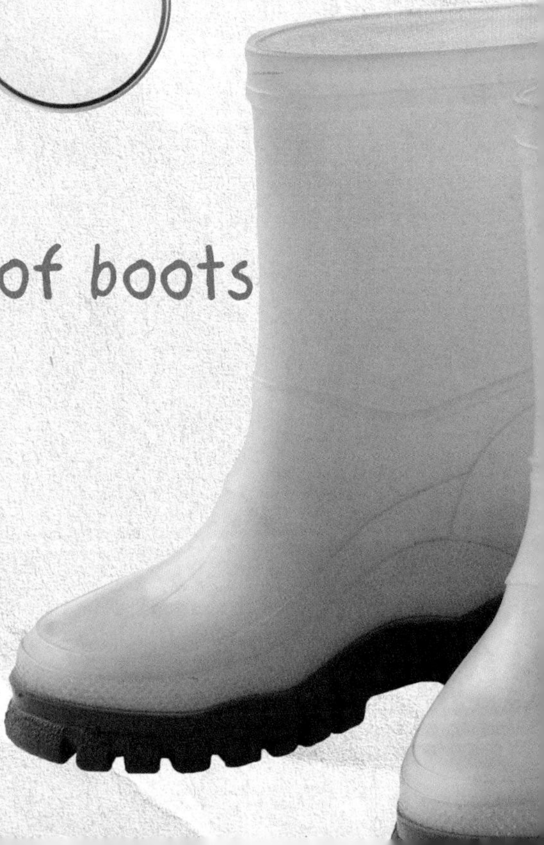

BE KIND!

It is important not to **disturb** wild creatures.

Keep your distance.

WHAT IS A BUTTERFLY?

Butterflies have four wings. They come in different shapes, sizes, and colors.

Butterflies are **insects**.

Butterflies can live in forests, fields, and even **sand dunes**.

How many butterflies can you see?

Whenever you see a hand, place your finger and thumb on the page to see how big the butterfly is.

Monarch butterfly

PEACOCK BUTTERFLY

Actual size

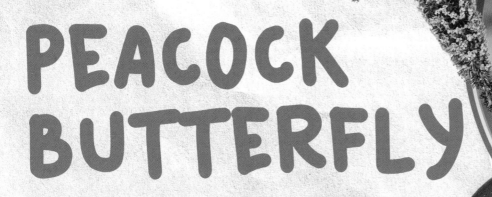

This colorful butterfly lives in woods, gardens, and parks.

Place your finger and thumb here

Peacock butterflies have eyespots that look like a peacock feather on them.

EMERALD SWALLOWTAIL BUTTERFLY

The emerald swallowtail butterfly has a green streak of color on its wings.

Actual size

Place your finger and thumb here

This butterfly's wings are shaped like the wings of a swallow.

TORTOISESHELL BUTTERFLY

These butterflies are often found in gardens near flowers like this one.

Actual size

Place your finger and thumb here

Tortoiseshell butterflies lay their eggs on plants called stinging nettles.

COMMON BLUE BUTTERFLY

These butterflies are found in shrub-covered fields, sand dunes, and **meadows**.

Actual size

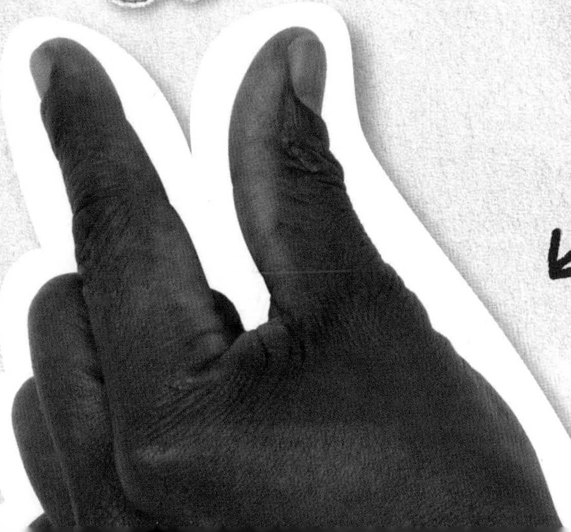

Place your finger and thumb here

Females have a spotty pattern on the underside of their wings.

How many spots can you count?

ORANGE-TIP BUTTERFLY

Actual size

The orange tips on the male butterflies tell **predators** that they do not taste nice!

Place your finger and thumb here

They have a green pattern that looks like moss on the underside of their wings.

COMMA BUTTERFLY

The comma butterfly has wings with jagged edges. These help it to **camouflage**.

Actual size

Place your finger and thumb here

It gets its name from the white comma shape on the underside of its wing.

BUTTERFLY PATROL

We have learned about butterflies that live around the world. How many other kinds can you spot where you live?

Peacock butterfly

Emerald swallowtail butterfly

Tortoiseshell butterfly

Common blue butterfly

Orange-tip butterfly

Comma butterfly

It's time to go... looking for butterflies!

GLOSSARY

camouflage to use things that an animal has that let it blend in and hide itself

disturb to move or touch

insects animals that have six legs and sometimes one or two pairs of wings

meadows areas with lots of grass

predators animals that eat other animals for food

sand dunes hills or ridges of sand made by the wind

INDEX